MR. TOPSY-TURVY

by Roger Hargreaves

WORLD INTERNATIONAL

Mr Topsy Turvy was a funny sort of a fellow.

Everything about him was either upside down, or inside out, or back to front – topsy turvy in fact.

It was all very extraordinary!

To give you some idea of how topsy turvy Mr Topsy Turvy was, you ought to see his house.

The front door is upside down to start with.

And the curtains hang upside down at the windows.

And just look at that chimney pot!

All very extraordinary!

Inside is the same.

Just look at the clock standing on Mr Topsy Turvy's mantelpiece.

Isn't that the topsiest turviest clock you've ever seen?

And just look at the way Mr Topsy Turvy reads a book.

Not only does he read it upside down, but he starts to read it at the back page!

MR BUMP
by Roger
MR BUMP

And just look where Mr Topsy Turvy puts the stamp when he sends a letter to somebody.

Have you ever seen anything like it?

Mr Smith
High Street
the Town

Now, this story is all about the time Mr Topsy Turvy came to the town where you and I live.

Nobody is quite sure how Mr Topsy Turvy got there, or where he came from, but he did arrive, because somebody saw him getting off the train.

The trouble was, he did it in a topsy turvy way, and got out the wrong side and fell on to the railway line.

Which really isn't all that surprising, is it?

When he'd picked himself up and managed to find his way out of the station, Mr Topsy Turvy went to a hotel to find a room to spend the night.

The hotel manager tried not to smile when he saw Mr Topsy Turvy walk into his hotel carrying his suitcase upside down and with his topsy turvy hat on his head.

"Good afternoon, sir," he said. "Can I help you?"

Now, something you didn't know about Mr Topsy Turvy is the way he speaks.

You see, he sometimes gets things the wrong way round.

"Afternoon good," said Mr Topsy Turvy to the hotel manager. "I'd room a like!"

The manager scratched his head. "You mean you'd like a room?" he asked.

"Please yes," replied Mr Topsy Turvy.

Eventually the hotel manager managed to work out what Mr Topsy Turvy was talking about, and he was taken up in the lift to a bedroom.

Then Mr Topsy Turvy unpacked his suitcase, put on his pyjamas, and went to bed.

He was rather tired after travelling from wherever he'd come from.

The following day Mr Topsy Turvy went round the town.

But what a fuss his going round the town caused.

He took a taxi from the hotel, but so confused the taxi driver trying to tell him where he wanted to go, the poor man drove straight into a traffic light.

"Oh dear," said Mr Topsy Turvy. "I am sorry very!"

TAXI

Then he went into a big department store in the middle of the town.

He walked up to one of the counters.

"I'd like a sock of pairs," he said to the lady behind the counter.

"You mean a pair of socks," she smiled, and showed him a pair of bright red socks.

Mr Tospy Turvy put them on his hands!

Then he tried to leave, but being Mr Topsy Turvy he tried to walk down the up escalator, and all the people who were going up the up escalator all fell over themselves.

It was a terrible topsy turvy jumble!

That day Mr Topsy Turvy did all sorts of topsy turvy things.

He walked backwards across a street crossing, and caused an enormous traffic jam.

He went to a library and put all the books upside down on the shelves, and made everybody extremely cross.

Then he went to an art gallery and insisted on hanging all the pictures upside down so that he could look at them properly.

And then, after Mr Topsy Turvy had been in the town for just one day, he disappeared.

Nobody knew how he went, or where he went, but he certainly went because he wasn't there any more.

The whole town breathed a sigh of relief.

But . . .

What the town discovered, even though Mr Topsy Turvy had left, was that everything was still topsy turvy.

"Read all it about," shouted the newspaper sellers, instead of shouting, "Read all about it".

"News is the here," said the television newsreader, instead of saying, "Here is the news".

"Morning good," people started saying to each other when they met, and "Do do you how?" instead of, "How do you do?"

Everybody was talking topsy turvy!

Can you think of something to say that's topsy turvy?

Go on, try!

•RETURN THIS WHOLE PAGE•

3 Great Offers For Mr Men Fans

1 FREE Door Hangers and Posters

In every Mr Men and Little Miss Book like this one you will find a special token. Collect 6 and we will send you either a brilliant Mr. Men or Little Miss poster and a Mr Men or Little Miss double sided, full colour, bedroom door hanger. Apply using the coupon overleaf, enclosing six tokens and a 50p coin for your choice of two items.

Egmont World tokens can be used towards any other Egmont World / World International token scheme promotions., in early learning and story / activity books.

Posters: Tick your preferred choice of either Mr Men ☐ or Little Miss ☐

Door Hangers: Choose from: Mr. Nosey & Mr Muddle ☐, Mr Greedy & Mr Lazy ☐, Mr Tickle & Mr Grumpy ☐, Mr Slow & Mr Busy ☐, Mr Messy & Mr Quiet ☐, Mr Perfect & Mr Forgetful ☐, Little Miss Fun & Little Miss Late ☐, Little MIss Helpful & Little Miss Tidy ☐, Little Miss Busy & Little Miss Brainy ☐, Little Miss Star & Little Miss Fun ☐. (Please tick)

2 Mr Men Library Boxes

Keep your growing collection of Mr Men and Little Miss books in these superb library boxes. With an integral carrying handle and stay-closed fastener, these full colour, plastic boxes are fantastic. They are just £5.49 each including postage. Order overleaf.

3 Join The Club

To join the fantastic Mr Men & Little Miss Club, check out the page overleaf NOW!

Allow 28 days for delivery. We reserve the right to change the terms of this offer at any time but we offer a 14 day money back guarantee. The money-back guarantee does not affect your statutory rights. Birthday and Christmas cards are sent care of parent/guardians in advance of the day. After 31/12/00 please call to check that the offer details are still correct.

•RETURN THIS WHOLE PAGE•

Join Our Club!

MR. MEN & little miss CLUB

When you become a member of the fantastic Mr Men and Little Miss Club you'll receive a personal letter from Mr Happy and Little Miss Giggles, a club badge with your name, and a superb Welcome Pack (pictured below right).

You'll also get birthday and Christmas cards from the Mr Men and Little Misses, 2 newsletters crammed with special offers, privileges and news, and a copy of the 12 page Mr Men catalogue which includes great party ideas.

If it were on sale in the shops, the Welcome Pack alone might cost around £13. But a year's membership is just £9.99 (plus 73p postage) with a 14 day money-back guarantee if you are not delighted!

HOW TO APPLY To apply for any of these three great offers, ask an adult to complete the coupon below and send it with appropriate payment and tokens (where required) to: Mr Men Offers, PO Box 7, Manchester M19 2HD. Credit card orders for Club membership ONLY by telephone, please call: 01403 242727.

To be completed by an adult

❑ **1.** Please send a poster and door hanger as selected overleaf. I enclose six tokens and a 50p coin for post (coin not required if you are also taking up 2. or 3. below).

❑ **2.** Please send __ Mr Men Library case(s) and __ Little Miss Library case(s) at £5.49 each.

❑ **3.** Please enrol the following in the Mr Men & Little Miss Club at £10.72 (inc postage)

Fan's Name:______________________Fan's Address:______________________________

____

______________________________Post Code:__________________Date of birth:___/___/___

Your Name:______________________Your Address:______________________________

____

Post Code:___________Name of parent or guardian (if not you):______________________

Total amount due: £_________ (£5.49 per Library Case, £10.72 per Club membership)

❑ I enclose a cheque or postal order payable to Egmont World Limited.

❑ Please charge my MasterCard / Visa account.

Card number: | | | | | | | | | | | | | | | | |

Expiry Date: _____/_____ Signature: ______________________

Data Protection Act: If you do **not** wish to receive other family offers from us or companies we recommend, please tick this box ❑. Offer applies to UK only